Time for Tom

by Phil Vischer

Tommy
NELSON™

Thomas Nelson, Inc.
Nashville

Art Direction:
Ron Eddy

3D Illustrator:
Aaron Hartline

Assistant 3D Illustrator:
Jeremy Vickery

Copyright © 1998
by Big Idea Productions

Illustrations Copyright © 1998
by Big Idea Productions

Published in Nashville, Tennessee, by Tommy Nelson™,
a division of Thomas Nelson, Inc.

Library of Congress Cataloging-in-Publication Data
Vischer, Phil.
    Time for Tom / by Phil Vischer.
        p.   cm.
    Summary: Follows Tom Grape through his day, as he gets up, brushes his teeth, eats lunch at school, plays outside, and performs other appropriate activities according to the time.
    ISBN 0-8499-1534-1
    [1. Time — Fiction. 2. Clocks and watches — Fiction. 3. Day — Fiction. 4. Grapes — Fiction. 5. Stories in rhyme.] I. Title.
PZ8.3.V74Ti   1998
[E] — dc21
                                        97-43454
                                          CIP
                                          AC

Printed in the United States of America

99 00 01 02 03 BVG 9 8 7

Dear Parent

We believe that children are a
gift from God and that helping
them learn and grow is nothing less
than a divine privilege.

With that in mind, we hope these
"Veggiecational" books provide years
of rocking chair fun as they teach
your kids fundamental concepts
about the world God made.

– Phil Vischer
President
Big Idea Productions

Bob and Larry are here today
To stage for you a little play.
So call your dad and get your mom —
It's time to start "It's Time for Tom!"

It's time for Tom
    to rise and shine.
The sun is up;
    he's feeling fine!

The bus will come at five till nine.
It's time for Tom to rise and shine.

It's time for Tom
    to make his bed
And fluff the pillow
    that holds his head

And smooth the sheet with the purple thread.
It's time for Tom to make his bed.

It's time for Tom
    to go to school
And learn about
    the golden rule

And sit at his desk
on a tiny stool.
It's time for Tom
to go to school.

It's time for Tom
to eat his lunch
With Laura and Junior,
his favorite bunch.

With things to drink, and things to munch,
It's time for Tom to eat his lunch.

It's time for Tom
   to play outside —
To run and jump
   and swing and slide,

With places for Junior
　　and Laura to hide!
It's time for Tom
　　to play outside.

It's time for Tom to eat again,
With Ma and Pa
  they sit and then

Thank God for their food with a big Amen!
It's time for Tom to eat again.

It's time for Tom to hit the tub.
From head to toe,
   he needs a scrub!

So get the soap and start to rub.
It's time for Tom to hit the tub!

It's time for Tom
to go to bed.
He's feeling tired —
his eyes are red.

He puts his nightcap on his head.
It's time for Tom to go to bed.

It's time for Tom
    to say his prayers.
He's thankful for
    a God who cares —

Who fills us up with the love He shares.
It's time for Tom to say his prayers.

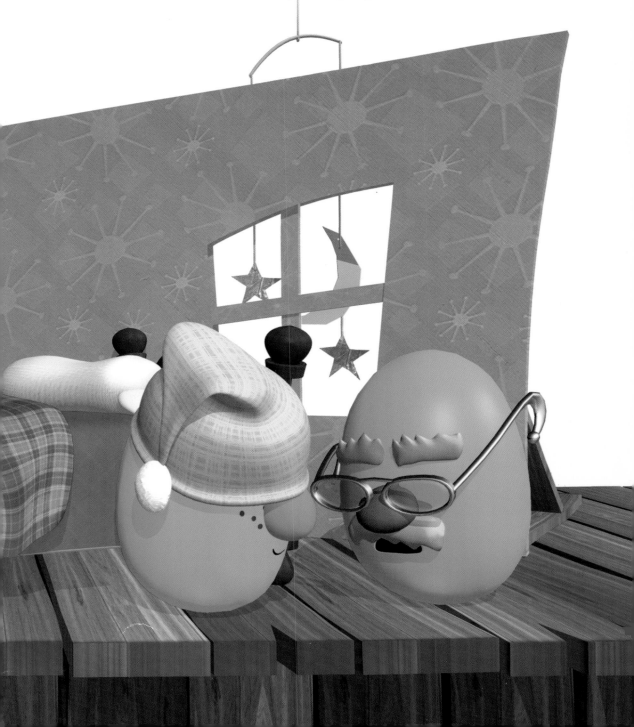

It's time for Tom
    to say good night.
Pa tucks him in —
    turns out the light.